The Black Flower

HOLDEN SHEPPARD

DEDICATION

This story is dedicated to the absolutely hammered guy who tried to speak to me about why he drank at the pharmacy that time, and whom I ignored by pretending to be on my phone.

It is also dedicated to anyone who has ever parked outside a bottle shop at eight o'clock in the morning, waiting for them to open.

ACKNOWLEDGMENTS

There are several people involved in this story reaching publication.

I wish to thank the team at Busybird Publishing, in particular Beau Hillier, editor of Melbourne literary anthology *page seventeen*, who saw the potential in this poignant, unsympathetic character, and published an earlier version of this story in 2015.

I also wish to thank the awesome Raphael Farmer, who beta-read this new version for me; Georgina Gregory of Plume, who did a fantastic copy edit (and had a wonderfully absurd conversation with me about sud-covered crotches); and my talented cover designer, Angie, who knocked it out of the park again.

The Black Flower

HOLDEN SHEPPARD

I hate my best mate.

I am so sick of him tilting his head to the side, frowning like a wanker as he judges me for passing out on his shitty blue sofa. 'Had one too many again, hey, Nick?' Little laugh. A work laugh.

Like, what does he think? I'm gonna have a little chuckle with him every day?

Firstly, I'm hungover and I'm not in the mood for some cheap-arse moron who smells like Woollies-brand hair gel to click his tongue at me.

Secondly, I don't give him that attitude. I don't shuffle into the brown-tiled bathroom behind him and comment on his life choices. 'What, you're wearing another creased white fifteen-dollar business shirt again today, Donny?' Tilt head. Little laugh. 'What, you're going to a soul-sucking intern job that you hate, just because your daddy got it for you? Whose fault is that, huh?'

He's the biggest prick in the world and, if I had any other mates left, I would've been outta here two weeks ago.

My mornings are now structured to avoid him altogether. If he wasn't such a wang, I'd sleep right through until the grog wore off, but his alarm clock is cranked up to nightclub volume and it plays that dubstep shit that sounds like robots giving each other blow jobs. I hear his crumby knife scrape on toast, his off-key rendition of some David Guetta song in the shower, his phone beeping as he taps out a few early morning emails. Sad bastard.

I wait until I hear his work shoes clap on the concrete outside, and the prissy hatchback's engine purr away, before I raise myself gingerly from the bed, like a vampire rising from a coffin – and just as thirsty.

I'm blinking, bleary, crook in the guts. But already something unmistakeable is happening in the pit of my stomach: excitement.

Excitement doesn't quite cut it, but I can't explain it much better. Even on mornings when the sun coming through the venetians pierces my eyes and my head is thumping like a wacker packer, I start thinking about that first sip and it starts to grow like a flower in my solar plexus. It gives me goose bumps. Kinda like being horny, but stronger than that. The more you think about it, the more you want it.

This morning, I'm champing at the bit by the time Donny locks the door and starts the hatchback's engine. I chuck the sheets off and stumble straight to the kitchen. You can tell where his side of the fridge ends and mine begins: there's shelves of kale and yoghurt and green juices, and then the crisper is chockas with my stuff: VB, Emu, Swan.

The early morning drinks.

Cold beer down my throat. I always scull the first one and feel the happy tingle in my stomach and the loving flush of my face.

Beers number two and three follow immediately. I'm better at Call of Duty when I've had a few to take the edge off. I lose track of time sitting on the beanbag with my arse going numb. Halfway through, I see a female civilian who kinda looks like Ash. I shoot her repeatedly with my Micro-Uzi. The game lets her live. You're not meant to shoot civilians. She keeps on strolling down the street, thirty-seven bullets having bounced off her bronzed skin.

I take beer number four out on the back patio with a

smoke. For me, it's the best part of the day: the sky still grey and pink, like a galah; the air crisp and cold; the smell of tobacco smoke mixed with grog. I hunch over the table and check the footy forums on my phone for the latest. There's nothing new.

'Nick.'

The voice electrocutes my nerves. Donny's standing at the door of the patio.

'Thought you left,' I say.

'Forgot these,' Donny says, holding a clump of documents. 'You just get home or what?'

'Nah, wasn't out.'

'You were home last night? I thought you were out.'

'Nah, was just in my room, man.' Avoiding your fat fucking face. Nursing a bottle of Wild Turkey until I passed out.

Donny looks at the nearly-empty stubby next to my phone. He looks upset for some reason. 'You gonna look for a job today or what, mate?'

I set my teeth on edge. I want to bite the red tie off his neck and strangle him with it.

'Oh yeah, bud,' I lie jovially. 'Got an interview later on. Still time for a coupla cold ones.'

Donny shakes his head. 'Mad dog,' he mutters. But it's different to how he used to call me 'mad dog' a week or two ago. I didn't know until now that there were two ways of saying that.

He jerks his head up by way of leave-taking and starts to slide the patio door shut.

But then it opens again, and he faces me. There's pink in his fat cheeks, like an undercooked steak.

'Nope,' he snarls suddenly. 'I'm so over this shit, Nick. I can't just watch this happen in front of my eyes.'

I wash down a lungful of tobacco smoke with the last of the beer. 'Watch what happen?'

'Get out. Get your crap outta my spare room and get out. By tonight. I don't wanna see you here when I get back.'

I feel my lip curling as I lock eyes with him.

'It's not your spare room, though, is it, Don? It's Daddy's.'

Donny snorts. 'Don't try that on, mate. He wants you here even less than I do.'

'Like that, is it?'

'Find somewhere else,' Donny says, fists balled.

'I've got nowhere else to go, man. What happened with Ashlea —'

'Christ's sake, I'm sick of hearing about Ashlea!' Donny snaps. He takes a breath and his shoulders droop. 'I'm sorry about it, Nick. I really am. But it's not my problem to live with. It's yours.' He turns around. 'I'll be home by six. Be out by then. Catchya.'

'You're a cunt, Don. I hate you.'

'I guarantee I hate you more, prick.'

#

Ashlea was the first girl I'd ever met who was worth sticking with. A wild-haired, wild-eyed surfer girl who could even give me a run for my money with the booze. We met at a house party in the older part of Seacrest, where she was doing a body shot off some other chick. We hooked up behind the garden shed that night, and somehow that turned into the first serious relationship of my life.

After we finished high school, I used to pick her up on my scooter and we'd go down to the town beach. She'd swim with her mates while I slipped beers from the esky. She'd come and watch me play footy on Saturdays, until I did my ankle. After that, she'd still sit with me through the Eagles games each weekend. Not bad at sussing out the odds, either, was Ash.

When we'd been together just over a year, her dad got sick. Some specific kind of cancer that heavy drinkers get.

I forget what it was called. But it went fast. In March, he was laughing at some Carl Barron stand-up on TV, swearing at us between cackles and telling us off for making out in the lounge room. In April, he was paper-thin and paper-white, eyes wide and empty, so exhausted in the middle of making a glass of bourbon and coke that he had to sit down.

And in May, he was gone.

All the wildness left Ash. A week after the funeral, she said to me, 'Nick, do you want to have kids?'

It was in the middle of Hawthorn demolishing us. Donny was next to me on the couch.

'Good way to give a bloke a heart attack,' I scoffed, nudging Donny. He laughed compliantly.

Ashlea sipped her white wine. 'Whatever.'

A couple of weeks later, she made dinner – steak – and it was just the two of us.

'I was seriously asking you the other day,' she said, tying her sun-bleached hair off her face. 'Do you want to have kids?'

'You mean like, one day?'

'Maybe now.'

I crushed my empty can of Emu and got up to get another one from the fridge.

'You for real? Ash, I'm still eighteen.'

'So? I am, too. Mum had me when she was eighteen.'

'Different generation.'

'Can you get your arse back to the table and have this discussion with me properly, please?'

The wildness had returned to Ashlea's pale eyes.

I cracked the beer and had a swig. 'No,' I said, turning my back to her as I wiped my mouth. 'I don't want kids.'

'Right now?'

'Ever.'

'You're just saying that to be a prick to me.'

Like a muscle reflex, my fist clenched around the nearly-full can of Emu. Metal crackled and buckled beneath my calloused hands. Cold amber fluid fizzed over my cracked skin and onto the linoleum. My ears were ringing, and it had nothing to do with the grog.

'No. I'm saying I never want kids,' I snarled. 'I don't want to bring kids into a world as shit as this.'

Ashlea was leaning back in her chair, like she was trying to put distance between us, even though I hadn't moved to threaten her or nothing.

The wildness had left her eyes again. She looked miserable.

'It's because of your dad, isn't it?' she whispered.

'Nothing to do with that son of a bitch,' I said, sucking beer off my fingers. 'Fuck staying in tonight. Let's go out to the Vibe.'

'I don't feel like clubbing.'

'So what? I do.'

Ashlea scraped her fork against the cheap plastic plate. 'I think you're drinking too much, Nick.'

#

After Donny goes off to work again, I swig the rest of the Wild Turkey until it's gone. Finally, the buzz is coming back. It takes so long to get it back nowadays. But now I'm craving more of the good stuff, and all I've got is beer.

I take the bare essentials out to the old Falcon: two mixed cartons of beer, ciggies, my jumper, my wallet and my phone. I leave most of my shit at Donny's. Stuff him. If he wants me out, I'm gone, but he can deal with cleaning up that room. I can't be arsed, and I've got nowhere to put anything anyway.

And I only have one destination in mind.

I pull my Eagles beanie on and fire the Falcon up. Takes three goes this morning: piece of crap's on its way out.

On my way to the bottle-o, a cop car pulls up next to me at a set of lights.

'Shit!' I say, forgetting my window is down.

The cop riding shotgun looks around: he's a blond bloke and looks like a deadset tosser. I feel my eyes getting sucked towards his, like bathwater circling the drain. I catch his gaze briefly before looking forward, gripping the steering wheel with two hands. I don't think I had two hands on it before. I stare at the traffic ahead of me and feel the cop's eyes burning on my cheek. Time passes like molasses. Then the light goes green and the cops zoom forward and I quickly chuck a left to get the hell away.

I get about a hundred metres down the road and just start cracking up. They had no idea I was half cut. And I've never seen anyone get breathalysed at eight on a bloody Tuesday morning.

I have to dog-leg through some back streets to get back on course but I still rock up at the local shopping centre before the bottle-o opens. The car park is devoid of human life: a few parked cars, weedy potholes in the old bitumen and a big sign with half the letters missing so it says 'Sun Pla'. I turn the ignition off, breathing on my hands and rubbing them together to warm them before lighting a smoke. And now I wait.

I wonder what I look like to other people as they drive past. Do they even notice the car parked outside the bottle-o at eight-thirty in the morning? Do they even wonder why it's parked there that early?

Just after twenty past, a young, blonde woman pulls up beside me in a battered white Barina. Her hair is a bird's nest and she's got no makeup on. She shoulders a nappy bag while trying to get her whinging baby out of the back.

I roll the window down. 'You need a hand?'

The woman jumps about ten feet into the air, glances around like a twitching mouse, then goes back to unstrapping her baby.

'I can hold your bag if you need,' I offer again. 'Or your baby. I'm great with kids. I can make 'em laugh real easy.'

This time she doesn't even turn around. She scoops her

baby up with one arm, not even supporting the head properly, and scampers away across the carpark.

'Rude bitch!' I yell out. 'Just tryin'a help!'

I get out of my car and light up another durry, but it doesn't even take the edge off. Sometimes a smoke isn't good for nothing. I wish I had more bourbon left in the bottle. I hate having to wait for booze.

I pace back and forth in front of the bottle-o. My head is thumping again. My hands are trembling. I look at my phone. Eight-thirty! Why aren't the shutters up? I knock on the shutter three times; the whole thing reverberates metallically and I wait, but nothing happens.

'Come *on*!' I shout through the shutter. 'Get your bloody acts together!'

Another five or ten minutes pass and there's no action. I bang on the shutters a few more times but nobody opens up. For fuck's sake.

I turn away from the shutters to light another smoke and I freeze in my tracks. The cops from the traffic lights have just pulled into the car park.

I freeze and lean against the shutters of the bottle-o, scrolling through my phone as casually as I can, glancing up every few seconds to track the paddy wagon. It creeps along the perimeter of the car park, way beyond the main shopping centre entrance, before pulling up right next to me.

The cops get out. The blond tosser is a beefy bloke and already seems real dark on me, smirking at me and puffing his chest out. The driver is a woman cop, a brunette, olive-skinned and dark-eyed. She actually has a killer rack, but all caged up in that blue police uniform it's a bit of a turn-off.

I look down at my phone and try to pretend they aren't there. At least I'm not driving.

The cops start to move, jangling loudly with their chains or keys, or whatever they have on them that makes that noise. The noise stops about three feet away from me. The sun is suddenly out of my eyes.

The bloke clears his throat and I look up. 'What are youse looking at, officers?'

'G'day mate, I'm Constable Adam White and this is my colleague, Constable Rosa Lopez. We've received a complaint from the staff here about a disturbance this morning. D'you know anything about that?'

'Nah, I haven't seen nothin'. They haven't even opened yet and it's quarter to nine.'

'This store opens at nine am,' says Constable Lopez.

'No kidding?' I say, looking at the little red sign beside the shutter. Son of a bitch. She's right.

'The store manager reported someone pounding on the door and yelling abuse at staff,' Constable White says. He crosses his arms. 'I think that mighta been you, mate.'

'Nah.' I shrug. 'I did knock on the shutters, but that's it, you know. Just tryin'a get a pressie for me dad's birthday. It's today. He likes bourbon.'

'Our report was that you threatened to smash these shutters in,' Constable White says.

'Piss off!' I cry. 'You can't just put words in my mouth. Jeez! I told you it wasn't me!'

'A male youth wearing ripped jeans, red ice hockey jersey and a beanie. Are you saying there're two of you hanging around this morning, mate?' Constable Lopez says. 'We need you to move along.'

'You cops are always pickin' on me!' I spit. 'I didn't do nothin'.'

'Move along,' White says.

'This is bullshit,' I say, moving for my car. 'Well, thanks a lot, my old man's not gonna get a birthday present thanks to youse. Happy now?'

'Keep moving,' White says, like a real wanker.

'Bloody pigs,' I mutter, loud enough for them to hear.

I get about two metres from my car when I realise I can't get behind the wheel or they'll do me for drink-driving. I change course and head for the shopping centre entrance. I look back over my shoulder and the cops are both still standing guard out the front of the bottle-o, arms crossed like complete tossers.

I pull the finger and I know they see it, but they don't move.

#

Sometimes there's nothing better than a shower beer. It makes getting ready for the clubs just a little more exciting – as long as you don't get the foam of Lynx shower gel mixed in with the foam of Swan Draught.

There was a thud at the bathroom door. It opened a crack. I could hear Donny and the boys laughing on the patio. Then the door shut.

'Nick,' Ashlea said.

I grinned and slid the opaque shower screen open. 'Told you you'd change your mind,' I said, grabbing a handful of my sud-covered crotch. 'Coming in?'

Grabbing my dick made me lose my balance; I nearly slipped, and flailed my hands out. Ashlea grabbed both hands and steadied me.

'Jesus,' I muttered, my face warm. The room was still spinning. 'Thanks babe. Floor's pretty slippery.'

'I bet that's what it is,' she said, picking at a bit of peeling skin on her sunburnt forearm.

'So, you want to –'

'Nick, I'm pregnant.'

'Huh?'

'I'm three weeks late. I did the test this morning. I've been freaking out. I didn't know how to tell you. I think it's from that time after the funeral. You didn't use a condom.'

The shower rained on my ears.

Ashlea started crying. 'I'm sorry.'

'Sorry ...' I echoed. Steam rushed against my face. My hand was leaning on the hot tap. I thought my skin was burning, but I could hardly feel it. 'Why? Is it mine?'

Her face soured and she slapped my arm. 'Of course it's yours!' she snapped.

'Why are you sorry then?'

'Because you don't want this.'

It felt like the water was spitting out of the shower head as scorching-hot needles. I shut the tap off and stood in front of Ashlea, every part of me dripping water, my dick limp.

I didn't feel anger. Not a shred of it.

'We could have a baby,' I muttered. I could barely hear my own voice. Maybe I was drunker than I'd realised.

Tears were streaming down Ashlea's cheeks. Green mascara rivulets.

'I don't know if I want to,' she muttered.

'Are you serious?' I fumbled for the VB-themed towel and wrapped it around my waist.

'I mean, because of you,' she said, crossing her arms and stepping back as I got out of the shower, beer clenched in hand. 'I know what it's like to grow up with a dad who won't stop drinking. I lost him. He was thirty-nine, Nick. That's not that old. And I know what you went through with your dad ...' She looked up at me, wet-eyed. 'I don't want to do this if you're going to go down the same road.'

Ironically, it was because I was plastered that I didn't feel angered by her accusation. I put my arms around her, flexed them tight, caging her within the heat of my chest, and tipped the beer out into the bathroom basin.

'I don't have a problem,' I said, pouring the can out until it's empty. 'I won't drink again. For you. For our kid.'

Ashlea sobbed and nestled closer into my wet skin. 'Thank you, Nick. Thank you.' She wiped her nose. Her whole body was shaking. 'I've been so worried. I didn't think you'd take it this well.'

I snorted. 'Neither did I.'

She breathed a stream of relief into my solar plexus. 'We're going to have a baby, Nick.'

#

'Fucken poxy shithole,' I curse as I walk into the shops. I figure I'll kill some time here 'til the cops piss off, then go back and get my bourbon.

I pace around Sunset Plaza, looking at the shops. The whole place is old and decaying. Half the lights don't work.

In the middle of the mall, there's one of those professional photographer set-ups. There's a queue of mums with their babies. The blonde chick I offered to help outside is in the line, her kid wriggling in her arms.

I shuffle past and peer over the photographer's partition. There's a pastel pink backdrop set up. The photographer's a brown girl with a strong English accent. She's fussing over a young couple and their two kids, perched on some quaint little chairs that don't look strong enough to hold their weight.

There's a guy in line for the photographer, holding hands with his son. The boy turns to his dad and mutters something in toddler gibberish. Nonsense.

But the dad stares at him, and nods along to each syllable. 'Really, Noah? That's awesome.'

I move on.

The food court is scummy: a bakery, an Indian takeaway place and a generic café. My guts are gurgling, but I can't afford to eat this early in the day. It'll kill my buzz and send me to sleep before I can get really out of it.

I pass by a cheap menswear shop. There's a bloke with a salt-and-pepper goatee getting a charcoal-grey suit fitted by a middle-aged woman. A teenage kid is next to him, must be about twelve or thirteen. He's wearing a suit jacket, too, but it's oversized, the sleeves hanging over his hands.

'Dad,' he's elbowing his father's side. 'Dad. Dad. Dad.'

The salt-and-pepper bloke breaks from his conversation with the woman. 'What is it, Jack?'

'It doesn't fit me. Look. I need a different one.'

'Ease up, turbo. That's why the lady's measuring us. They'll alter it.'

'Oh.' The kid is legitimately relieved. 'Good. I don't wanna look stupid at the wedding.'

'Don't worry,' the dad says. 'I wouldn't let you rock up looking anything less than dapper.'

'Are you alright there?' the middle-aged woman calls over to me.

'Yeah. Fine. Why?' I mumble.

'We only sell suits here,' she says, squinting at my jersey.

'Yeah, so? Maybe I want a suit.'

She sighs. 'I'll be with you in a minute, then, sir.'

I flick my hand through the racks of grey suits. It's cheap. The kind of place Donny would go to get his work clothes. I flip through dozens of suits and business shirts, not seeing any of them.

My eyes are on the dad teaching his son how to do his tie up. Patiently taking him through the steps. And when the kid screws up, the dad just says, 'Okay, bud, let's try that again.'

#

The first time my father hit me, it started as an arm wrestle.

I was fifteen and I'd gone to Puck's Gym with Donny, whose uncle owned the place and was a bit of a local boxing personality. We rode there on our bikes after school one day in the summer term. We mucked around with a punching bag and took turns knocking each other around with paw-like red padded gloves. Then we grabbed some icy poles from the kiosk at the public swimming pool and Donny bit with his teeth into the sugared ice which always made my skin crawl. That sound. That sensation. Second only to blackboard nails.

Once it started getting dark, we lit up our ceremonial last cigarettes for the day and smoked them next to the skate park. Then Donny rode up the highway to Waggrakine and I rode down to Rangeway.

When I got back to our house on Rifle Range Road there was a bunged-up Nissan out the front. You could tell it had been painted white when it was first made but it now had that yellowy, twenty-year-grime look about it, like pale, undercooked custard.

Anyway, I shat myself, because I thought Mum had one of her dropkicks over at the house and had forgotten that Dad was coming home tonight.

I pushed the whiny flywire door open and prepared for a barney with Mum – she could be a real stubborn bitch, despite everything – but the lounge room TV was already flicked onto the cricket. Dad had his fat, scungy feet on the brown glass coffee table, clipping ugly, outsized toenails, dangerously close to a half-full glass of Wild Turkey.

'Don't say anything about the car,' he grunted. 'Don't start.'

I was happy to veer around him. Mum was on the sofa in the living room, the six o'clock news reflecting on her blank irises.

'Nick, darling,' she droned, long and baritone. 'You could've said you were running late, love.'

So this was one of those days when we were pretending she wasn't baked like a soufflé.

'Did you and Dad have a blue?' I prodded.

The line of her mouth crinkled.

'The car outside. Whose is it? Did he see?'

'Oh, that.' The crinkle lifted to the sky. 'No, it's his.' A genuine smirk split her wrinkles. 'They laid off twenty blokes from Daybreak. Including him.'

'So he sold the Clubsport?'

Mum lolled a bit on the sofa, her head spooling back like she'd just been boxed around the ears, but there was a dumb grin on her face. 'He had to.'

Trust her to take Dad getting the sack as a victory for her. I hated him for spending the cash on the car instead of the house, or us, but it seemed a bit deranged for her to actually celebrate the end of our cash flow.

'Has he got another job?'

'No, love.'

'Is he gonna look, but?'

'No. Says we'll live off the sales of the car for a few weeks.'

'Are you gonna get one?'

'One what?'

'A job, Mum.'

She picked at a loose edge of the sofa's armrest. A little cloud of stuffing popped out and floated to the sticky carpet.

'Can't, love. My depression.' The usual cough, like she was convincing me of her illness. 'You're old enough to get a job now, you know.'

'School,' I grunted. I hated it, but it was a good shield when Mum started getting creative like that.

'Where were you this arvo, then?'

'Went to Donny's uncle's gym.'

That was the moment Dad thundered into the kitchen looking to refill his bourbon.

'What're you going to a gym for?'

'Just doing some boxing with Donny.'

'Boxing,' Dad grunted. He puffed his chest out, his nipples hard beneath his white singlet. 'Think you're gettin' tough, do ya?'

Mum pretended to watch the news.

'We were just mucking around,' I said.

Dad slammed his elbow down onto the corner of the kitchen bench, holding one hand out open-palmed, beckoning for my grasp.

'You think you're stronger than me?' he grunted.

'No.'

'Let's test it.'

'I don't want to.'

'Get your arse up here.'

I got up, crossing in front of mum's line of vision as I went. She didn't react.

Dad put a hand behind his head. 'Come on. How slow are ya?'

I mirrored my father, clasping his fat, sweaty palm in mine. He squeezed it, crushing the bones in my hand. I flinched, but said nothing.

'Ready,' he said. 'Set. Go.'

I strained, using all my strength to try to put his arm down. It was immediately clear I didn't have a shot in hell. Dad might've been fat, but there was muscle underneath the flab. I grunted, pushing hard, while Dad leered at me, not even breaking a sweat.

I don't know what came over me, but knowing I was going to lose made me want to win somehow. I removed my left hand from behind my head and grabbed onto our grappling palms. Quickly, before Dad could react and use more force, I used all my strength in both arms to slam his hand down on the bench.

'Ha!' I cried. 'I win!'

Dad's fist cracked through the cartilage of my nose. My vision flashed black and white, pain shooting through my face.

'You are not stronger than me!' Dad roared, twisting his fingers through my hair and yanking hard. 'Say it!'

I couldn't see him through the flashing lights.

'Say it!'

'I'm not stronger than you,' I spluttered thickly, through the flow of warm blood from my nose.

'Cheating little cunt,' Dad snarled, throwing me head-first across the room. 'You're not going to the gym again. We can't afford it.'

I heard him pour another large glass of bourbon. He cleared his throat and stalked back to the lounge room to watch the cricket.

The return of my vision coincided with the pain in my nose getting worse.

'Mum,' I muttered, so Dad wouldn't hear. 'He hit me. Did you see that?'

She stared at the weather girl. 'You shouldn't have cheated, love. Remember, he lost his job today. He's not in a good place.'

It took half a tissue box before my nose stopped streaming. Dad was still watching the cricket. Mum was glued to a soap.

I spotted the bottle of Wild Turkey still perched on the kitchen bench. Without even thinking it through, I went over, opened the bottle and poured some into a glass.

'Don't,' Mum said.

'Why not?'

'Just don't.'

'Like you're gonna do anything to stop me,' I spat, swirling the bourbon around the glass before knocking it back.

It burned, but not as much as the pain.

#

After the middle-aged woman at the suit shop threatens to call security on me, I move towards the far end of the plaza, drifting in a warm, alcoholic daze. I slump onto a wooden bench.

'Hi there! You look like you could use some relaxation.'

I turn around to see a girl about my age. She's a petite Asian girl in a red and white polo shirt.

'What?'

'Do you want a massage? We can do a back massage with oil today for forty dollars. It's on special.'

I stare at her for about twenty seconds before realising that I'm sitting in front of a tiny massage parlour. Huh. Maybe a rub 'n' tug would do me good until the cops bugger off.

'Okay,' I say.

She waves me into the parlour, and palms me off to an older woman who doesn't speak much English. Panpipe music is playing. The air smells both sweet and savoury. The older masseuse beckons me into a curtained-off cubicle with a long wooden table. She puts a wicker basket on the table.

'Clothes in here. Keep pants on. Okay?' She draws the curtain.

Keep pants on – sure, lady. I strip down to my jocks and lay face down. Immediately beneath my face is a little cactus plant.

A little voice says, 'Okay, you ready?'

'Mm hmm,' I mutter.

She enters. 'No, no, pants on!' she chides.

She covers my arse with a towel and begins squirting cold oil on my back. Her hands glide over my back muscles, thumbs crunching the knots in my back with the force of a man.

I suddenly realise, with a surge of disappointment, that this is a legit massage joint. I'm not gonna be copping a hand job today. There's a checkout scanner from the supermarket bleeping in the background. Someone in the back of the parlour is trying to get a baby to sleep.

'My new grandson,' the Chinese masseuse apologises, then adds something in angry Mandarin to someone on the other side of the curtain. The baby's crying disappears out a back door. 'Two week old.'

'Congrats,' I say. I'm not fully drunk, not by a long shot, but my tongue is loosened enough to blurt out, 'You're lucky. My girlfriend was pregnant. Before …'

'Ah, you have baby, too? But you so young!'

'Nah – she …' The words die in my throat as the lump swells.

'Boy or girl?' the masseuse asks. We aren't having the same conversation.

'Boy.'

'Oh, so nice! What his name?'

'Um. Daniel.'

I feel the tingle in my gut again, the urge to obliterate stronger than ever. Unwanted tears drip onto the little cactus plant below my face: useless salt water that won't even nourish the plant.

'Pressure okay?' the masseuse asks.

'Uh huh.'

I close my wet eyes, but all I can think of is my son.

#

After Ashlea fell pregnant, I decided to sort my shit out and get a job. The only good work going was as a labourer with Main Roads, but it was out woop woop – they were bitumising an old gravel road past Mount Magnet. The money was sick. Sleeping in a donga in Magnet wasn't so fun, but it made the return to Geraldton, and to Ashlea, all the more sweet each month.

The fifth time I came back from Magnet, she texted me to say she would be out to dinner when I got home.

It was a trap.

I stumbled into our shitbox flat in Spalding in the dark. I hadn't brushed my teeth or had a chewy, because why would I need to? Ashlea was meant to be out.

Except the moment I flicked the light on, there she was, sitting bolt-upright on the sofa, her arms crossed fiercely over her belly.

Her eyes flicked to the bottle of Woodstock under my arm, and then my guilty, unshaven face.

'You said you were gonna be out,' I said.

'You said you'd quit drinking,' Ashlea snarled. 'Five months ago.'

She stood up and stalked over to my side, sniffing the air around my face. 'How many drinks did you have on the bus home?'

'Five,' I said at once. I smiled. It was out of guilt, and inebriation.

'I knew it,' she said coldly. 'I thought I smelled it on your breath last time you came home, but I didn't want to believe it.' She paced across the room. 'Did you even go a single day without a drink when you promised to give it up? Or have you been lying to me the whole time?'

I grinned back at her: a sick, unstoppable grin. I felt strangely proud, defying her.

'I went one day,' I said. 'The day after I promised I'd quit, I didn't touch a drop. And then the next day, Donny invited us boys around and, well, y'know?' I laughed. 'I drank every day, and you never even noticed, because I hid it so well.'

'I can never trust you again. You have a problem, Nick. Admit it. You have a problem.'

'Ash … you're so fucking lame now,' I spat. 'What happened to the girl who used to do body shots and flaming sambucas?'

'I grew up, Nick!' Ashlea cried. 'Can you? Please, seriously, can you grow up?'

'You're making such a big deal out of nothing,' I said. 'Everyone drinks this much. *Everyone.* All the blokes on the job do. All my mates here do.'

'That doesn't mean you don't have a problem!' Ashlea cried. 'That just means you're all fucked!'

She grabbed her suitcase from the sofa and tried to push past me.

'What the fuck?' I growled. 'Where do you think you're going?'

'I'm going to stay with my mum,' she said, mascara flowing. 'I need to think things over.'

'What is there to think over?' I said, grabbing her wrist and blocking her path. 'You're carrying my son. You're not leaving me.'

'Maybe you've left me with no choice, Nick.'

'You won't take him away from me,' I said stiffly. 'He's

the only good thing I've ever done.'

The mascara was streaking faster now.

'I think you're actually right,' Ashlea said softly.

She tried to push past me again, and instinctively, I squeezed her wrist. I heard the bones crunch in her hand.

'Ouch! You're hurting me, Nick! Stop!'

Rage erupted from nowhere; I released her wrist and slammed both hands into her chest, shoving her, hard. She skidded across the tiles and slammed against the wall.

Ashlea's eyes were wide with horror. She'd barely kept her feet. 'Move,' she whispered.

I shifted from the doorway and she strode through it, suitcase in tow. I'd taken my first swig of bourbon before she started the engine of her Excel.

Ashlea ignored my texts for three days. Her mum wouldn't answer the door when I drove around.

On the fourth day, she sent me a text message:

> Got rid of it yesterday. Couldn't raise a kid by myself and I'm not gonna raise a kid around a drunk violent deadbeat FUCK like you if you WON'T STOP DRINKIN!!!!

> You killed him, Nick. Not me.

I called her thirty times with no answer. I was drunk at the time, and my heart was racing. I screamed. I cried. I punched a hole in the door. My knuckles bled and I didn't care.

He could've been anything. He could've done more than me. Better than me. But he didn't make it, because of his fucked-up dad. Because of me.

He was the only flicker of light I had before he got snuffed out. I don't know how it happened, but I imagine him swimming around in Ashlea's womb, this happy little dude, and then the drugs kicking in and his little heart stopping and him floating to the top, like a dead fish.

\#

The masseuse works some magic on me. I fall asleep at some point; I only know this because I suddenly awaken to a sharp smack on my head.

'Ouch! What the hell?'

'Out – you go, get out now!' the Chinese lady squawks.

I get up, confused. An odour catches my nostrils. It smells like the massage oil went rancid. It's not until I feel the warm moisture in my jocks that I understand.

'Naughty boy – out, go!' the masseuse cries.

I don't say anything. I throw my jeans on, forgetting my shirt, and walk out of the massage parlour numbly, pee trickling down my legs. Not my fault. Coulda happened to anyone.

I walk into the carpark. The cops are gone. I gravitate to the open bottle-o and buy a bottle of cheap bourbon. I get into the passenger's seat of the Falcon but my gut is already tingling in anticipation. The black flower blossoms in my chest. No time to go home. I need it now.

I am shirtless. I am soaking wet with my own piss. I twist the cap off the bourbon and slide the brown paper down. My numb lips quiver, searching for the warm glass neck and finally locking around it.

I suck on my bottle and drink until I am empty.

Bonus Short Story

A Man

HOLDEN SHEPPARD

Originally published in Indigo Journal, *Volume 3*

Three forty-four. The phone screams. Who? Why? At this time? I throw my hand onto the bedside table. Nope, that's the wallet. Bit more to the right. Nope. Sunnies. Nope. Keys to the shed. Nope. Photo of Nat and me at Christmas. Ah. Smooth plastic. The phone. Hello? Missus who? No, I don't remember putting your leach drains in four months ago. What? Well, how is that my fault? It's the middle of the bloody night, ring back at seven. Then call *them* if they're better at it! I don't care. Let me fucking sleep!

5:16. Disentangle myself from Nat's warm body. No, honey, everything's fine. No, I just need to take a leak. Throw off the Egyptian cotton sheets she made me buy her. Cold. Cold. Cold air. Cold bathroom tiles. Clumsy path to the dunny. It takes a while to piss cause I've got the usual morning boner. I half lapse into sleep again while I stand over the bowl. I yawn, grunt, wash my hands, stub my toe on the edge of the doorframe and fall back into bed.

Half five. Alarm spews breakfast radio shit at me. Wrestles me out of bed. No, babe, nothing's wrong. Just gotta get up for work. Work. Fucking work. I pull on my boxers and stumble through the dark house. Dark passage, dark kitchen. Dark laundry. My work clothes, still on the floor where I left them last night. I forgot Nat wants me to wash them myself now. Shit. I hold up the fluorescent yellow shirt. Sniff sniff. Yesterday's sweat. Yesterday's acrid grease. The blue pants are no better. Grease. Sand. Sweat.

Quarter to. A trail of sand follows me from the laundry to the kitchen. I reek, but there's nothing else for it. The other pair of work clothes is still on the line. I cover three Weet-Bix with 99% fat free milk. Haven't had full cream since Nat moved in.

Dawn. The truck won't start. It's a cold morning. I glow it again. It gives a weak cough and splutters out. On the fourth go the engine roars and we're off. Past the half-acre lots with cream-brick houses. Down Barrett Street, to the industrial estate. Stop at old Barney's Deli. How's it goin Barney. See the Eagles got flogged last night? Bet ya a carton youse don't make the eight now. Haha. Yeah, just the *West* and an iced coffee. Cheers, mate. Seeya s'arvo.

Ten past six. Third best part of the day. I'm always first to the yard. I throw the padlocks off the old metal gates and charge up the gravel driveway in third gear. I park the truck behind the big shed. The sun's in my eyes but not too much. I sit, turn the radio up a fraction. *Rock and Roll Ain't Noise Pollution*. Sweet iced coffee. Sport section. Fraser's still out with a shoulder injury. Wood's been suspended so he's out of the ruck too. Fuck.

Work. John's ute rolls up in a cloud of gravel dust. Reckon he takes the driveway in fifth ay. Gives me a nod and goes to open the shed. Last drop of cold coffee. Chuck it to the floor of the truck. Jump out. Fifteen steps over the metal dust. Into the shed. How's it goin John. Want the *West*? Righto. OK. Right in town? No worries. I'll bring the truck. Seeya there.

Seven. Fucked if I can find anywhere big enough to park the truck in the main street. Ah, that spot in front of the bakery looks alright. Should squeeze in OK … Shit. Kerbage. Sounded rough. Ah well. She'll be right.

7:01. Hello? Hey babe. What's wrong? What? Mrs Bailey? Oh yeah, I told her to call back. Her leach drains? I don't remember ay. There's a file in that big cardboard box in the wardrobe, it's got all my paperwork in it. Can ya just have a look through it and see if you can find the job I did for her then? Mm. Yeah, I know you've gotta get ready for work but – OK – OK – thanks. Thanks babe. You're a legend.

Twenty past. Witch's hats surround me. It's not gonna be a long job, probably just today. Just gotta dig a shortish trench. Chuck in a coupla conduits to link together the two pipes we laid last week. Some new thing for the council. CCTV or some shit. John's still on his way. He had to call past the depot and run something past the foreman. Spose I'll just wait.

Half seven. Fuck this is boring.

7:35. Bakery smells good. Sausage rolls straight out of the oven. Warm jam donuts. Sugary apple slices with piles of fresh cream on em. Pretty blonde behind the counter. Looks about twenty. Nice rack. How's it goin. Nah, I already had brekkie, cheers. Youse got a dunny I could use?

Dunny. Iced coffee goes straight through me.

Ten to eight. John rocks up in his truck. He parks it on the other side of the road. Brakes screech. Runs the kerb more than I did. Front wheels are completely up on the footpath. Mad cunt.

Cutting. Sparks fly out from the blade of the road cutter. I hold the ten-litre watering can closer and cool the blade. The orange sparks die, but smoke and dust are still rushing up into the air. The roar is almost unbearable. You're meant to wear earplugs when you're this close to the saw but we don't have any. Don't think it makes a difference anyway. John swivels the cutter around and starts the next cut through the bitumen.

Half eight. I'm greasing up John's mini-excavator when a car horn blasts right next to me. I'm about to pull the finger at whoever the prick is when I see it's Nat. She's pulled up in her green Excel on the other side of the road, next to the truck. Waving me over. She's got a bit of paper in her hand. John gives me a nod. I put the grease gun on the excavator tracks and run over to Nat, dodging traffic. Hey babe. What? Oh, you're a legend. So I did do her leach drains then. Cheers for that. Yeah, I know you're in a rush. K. Have a good day at the branch, babe. Love you too.

Work. John scratches the gravel underneath the bitumen with the big metal teeth on the excavator's bucket. I stand back and lean on my shovel. If there's a rock or a dead pipe, I'll need to have a dig around. But there isn't.

Smoko. About time. The smell from the bakery's only been getting stronger over the last half an hour. Pretty blonde's still behind the counter. Hows it goin. Yeah, just a sausage roll thanks. Yeah, one of the plain ones on the top rack. (Top rack alright.) And sauce and a coke. No worries. Smells good. Tastes even better. Beef. Fuck being a vegetarian. Wash it down with coke. Quick piss in the bushes on the empty block behind the bakery. Back to work.

10:04. Dig. John's run into a heap of old copper pipes crossing the trench. All dead, but we gotta dig around em. Or, *I* do. Sweat's stinging my eyes. Arms are cooking and darkening. Hair's wet under the old Akubra. Shovel, shovel. Mute smell of damp sand. *Clang.* Dead pipe. *Tsunk.* Clean sand. *Clang. Tsunk.*

11:27. More pipes. Dig. *Clang. Tsunk.*

Lunch. Nat's branch isn't that far from the job. Figure I'll say g'day to her at least. Have lunch. The main street's busy. It's Fridey. Even the bank looks packed. I step into the aircon. Shit. There's a fair queue. Ah, there's Nat. She looks real professional in her red top and black jacket. Might give her a wave. Hey babe. Hm. She looks busy. Might have to wait in line then.

12:06. And wait.

12:10. And wait. Oh, nah, you can serve someone else, I'm just here to see Nat. No worries.

12:11. Hey babe. What, how was that embarrassing? Mm. Just came to see if ya wanted to get some lunch, cause I'm just down the road today. Not till one thirty? That's a pretty late lunch. Mm. Fair enough, yeah. Righto. Seeya tonight then, babe.

Quarter past. Hows it goin. Yeah, back again. Yeah it was good. Might get a pie this time though. Beef thanks. No sauce. Yeah, another coke. Ha! Reckon it's warm in here? How bout we trade jobs then? Haha. Righto. Catchya later. I step outside the bakery. John's sittin on a milk crate on the footpath, just inside the witch's hats. Good sausage rolls here ay John? Haha. Yeah, she's got a fucken big rack ay? Fucken oath. So we just gotta lay them last two pipes, glue em in, fill the trench and we're done. Gravel or metal dust? Right. I'll get a load from the yard later and bring it back here.

Half twelve. Jump back into the trench. John puts the conduits on the edge. I take the orange one and put it on the bottom of the trench. Make sure there's no sand inside the rim. Right. Chuck us the glue, John. Cheers. Fuck that reeks. Just about gettin high off it already. I brush a smear of blue glue around the ends of the conduits and shove em together. Right. Chuck us the other pipe.

Ten to one. Dig. I sink the shovel into the pile of cleanish sand. Gotta cover the pipes well before we chuck the gravel on. Fucken hot now. Sweat's stinging my eyes. Arms are cooking and darkening. Hair's wet under the old Akubra. Shovel, shovel. Mute smell of damp sand. *Tsunk.* Clean sand. *Tsunk.* Clean sand. *Tsunk.*

One o'clock. *Tsunk.*

Wacker. My bones vibrate as I push the wacker packer over the trench, compacting the sand. One, two, three, four times.

1:34. Nat'll be on lunch now. Wonder if she'll come past and say g'day.

Quarter to. I glow the truck. Get him on the first go. *Clunk.* Off the kerb. Crank the radio. *Khe Sanh.* Chug down the main street, windows down. Off to the yard for a load of gravel.

2:35. The excavator bucket scrapes against the truck's metal tray. Worse than nails on a blackboard. John scoops up a bucketful of gravel and swings the boom around one-eighty. I stand back. He shakes the orange gravel into the nearly full trench. I walk over the loose gravel in my shoes. Compact it down a bit.

2:36. John scoops up a bucketful of gravel and swings the boom around one-eighty. I stand back. He shakes the orange gravel into the nearly full trench. I walk over the loose gravel in my shoes. Compact it down a bit.

Twenty to three. I lug the wacker back over the trench. Bones vibrate. One, two, three, four times over.

Sweep. John loads the machine up onto his truck. I grab the big broom and sweep the gravel dust and shit off the road, back into the trench. Day over.

Half three. I pull the truck into the yard. Park it beside John's. Wipe my forehead. Fucken hot one today. Woulda got to forty easy. Wouldn't mind a few stubbies. It's Fridey anyway. I jump outta the truck. Fifteen steps over the metal dust. Into the shed. Grab a six-pack of Draught from the old fridge. Fuck it. I grab another one. Catchya Mondey, John.

Twenty to. Chuggin down Barrett Street. Stop at old Barney's deli. How's it goin Barney. Yeah, not bad ay. Just a little job for the council. Nah, we'll still flog 'em. Chuck young Richards in the ruck and we'll be right I reckon. Yeah, just the milk. Cheers, mate. Seeya Mondey.

Four o'clock. Second best part of the day. I sit down on the concrete porch. Take me boots off. Crack open the first stubby.

Beer. Cold. Cold beer. Cold and crisp and bitter. Perfect end to a hot day. Perfect end to the week. I rest my forearms on my knees and look around the front yard. The palms are dying. Have been for ages. Should probably water them, but it never makes any difference. The land's too dry for them here anyway. Still, they hold on pretty well. Still a bit of green at the centre of some of the leaves. I sit and watch the other people in the street coming home from work. The sheila across the road rocks up in her silver Camry and gives us a wave. Forgotten her name but I wave back. Grab another stubby. Ah. Even if it's a bit warmer, it's still beer. I chug it back. It's a good drop, Draught. I look over at my red ute. Fuck, it's needin a wash already. Should do that this weekend. Should keep it in good order. Might need to sell it soon. Shit. Shit shit shit. I sink the stubby and grab a third. Fourth. Fifth. Sixth. Second six-pack. Warm beer. It's not so bad once you get used to it, I spose. Mm. Just takes getting used to, that's all. The metal dust crackles as Nat's green Excel rolls up beside my ute. She looks upset. Her face is red. Hey babe. How was your – never mind. She steps over me on the porch, opens the door and goes inside without a word. I wait a second and decide to follow. Fuck. Didn't feel them beers till I got up.

Dusk. I drop my daks and shirt in the laundry and walk down to the bathroom in my jocks. The water's running. I don't need to knock. Warm air. Wet air. The fan's whirring loud. Hey baby. I know she won't say anything back. Her face is already streaked with blue mascara as she looks at her reflection. Like every other night. I move in behind her. Put my head on her shoulder. Kiss her ear. I rub the belly. It's getting big now. Only three months to go. Hey. It'll be alright, babe. Hey. It'll be alright. It's gonna be so good.

Best part of the day. Hot water on her lips.

Tea. Steak and vegies. Cauliflower, carrot, peas and mashed potatoes. Bottled tap water for her. Eighth stubby for me. Nat puts on some Fleetwood Mac in the background while we eat. During *Tusk* she looks at me and nearly smiles.

8:49. Mobile vibrates in my pocket. Dave and them blokes are goin to the pub to watch the footy again. I text back some shit about copping a root off the missus. Nat shifts on my lap and turns the volume up on *Miss Congeniality*.

Nine. Hello? Who? Mrs Bailey? Yeah. Yeah I got your message. Mm, but it's nine o'clock on a Friday night! Yeah I know I did your leach drains four months ago. Mm. OK. Look, give us a call first thing Mondey mornin, orright? Yeah, I'll sort it out. I will. Cheers. Bye.

9.15. Fuck. I'm buggered ay.

Half ten. "Babe. Wake up. The movie's over. Come on. Let's go to bed," says Nat.

Ten forty-four. Haven't pissed yet. Shit. Off the couch. Nat must've gone to bed already. Drunken path to the dunny. Half lapse into sleep again while I stand over the bowl. I yawn, grunt, wash my hands and stub my toe on the edge of the doorframe. Nail on my big toe looks like it cracked but there's no pain. Ten stubbies. I fall into bed beside Nat, head swirling. Fuck. I'm gonna feel this tomorrow.

ALSO BY HOLDEN SHEPPARD

The Scroll of Isidor (Short Story)

Levin Ruck was once a great warrior mage: the battle-scarred wartime hero of the alpine village of Dervine and defender of the Kingdom of Flaran. But with peacetime stretching into its seventh year, opportunities for action have been scarce – even in his role as Deputy Chief of the village.

So when Desma the orchard keeper rides in late one night with news of ominous noises in the mountains, Lev knows the time for action has come.

But when Chief Magnus refuses to act, Lev takes matters into his own hands. Defying orders, he and Desma ride to the mountains to investigate the source of the disturbance.

What they discover is beyond their worst fears: a deadly threat has arrived on the village's doorstep – and Lev and Desma are Dervine's first and only line of defence.

THE SCROLL OF ISIDOR is available in paperback.

It is also available as an e-book from Kindle, Barnes & Noble, Apple (iBooks), Kobo, Smashwords and more.

ABOUT THE AUTHOR

Holden Sheppard is a Perth-based YA and fantasy author originally from Geraldton, Western Australia. His short fiction has been published in *Indigo Journal* and *page seventeen*. He has also written for the *Huffington Post*, the *ABC*, *DNA Magazine* and *FasterLouder*.

A graduate of Edith Cowan University's Creative Writing program, in 2015 Holden was awarded a prestigious ArtStart grant from the Australia Council for the Arts. The following year, he undertook a mentorship through the Australian Society of Authors, developing his debut novel. He is a committee member of the Peter Cowan Writers' Centre in Joondalup.

In 2017, Holden began releasing his short stories as eBooks: titles including THE BLACK FLOWER, THE SCROLL OF ISIDOR and A MAN are available through Amazon, iBooks, Barnes & Noble, Kobo and Smashwords.

Holden is a discordant confluence of identities: a geeky rocker; a bogan who learned to speak French; and a gym junkie who has played Pokémon competitively. He may be the only writer to switch to decaf and live to tell the tale, and he's quit smoking more times than he cares to admit.

CONNECT WITH THE AUTHOR

Want to keep up to date with the latest news and releases from Holden Sheppard?

You can find him on the web and social media at the following coordinates:

Visit Holden's official website:
holdensheppard.com

Like Holden's page on Facebook:
facebook.com/HoldenSheppardAuthor

Follow Holden on Twitter:
twitter.com/V8Sheppard

Check out and follow Holden's blog:
holdensheppard.wordpress.com

Favourite Holden's Smashwords page:
smashwords.com/profile/view/holdensheppard

Follow Holden on Goodreads:
goodreads.com/holdensheppard